Time of Death

SUHANI GOYAL

*To August, the month that started it all; and
November, the one that ended it.*

Contents

SUMMER

AUTUMN

Winter

December

12:11 AM

Mid-December, my birthday wish wasted on you
I called, you came, love our eternal curse
I tried to erase it; tried to clear fogged up glass
And yet, wintry breath prevailed, all clarity lost

You clutch your pain close to your heart
You hold onto it like an arcane promise
And yet; some promises were made to break
Just as some love was born to die

I steal away your pain as you stole my promises
I hold that promise close like a secret
I let it fall from me till it dissipates
Like fragments of ice in pretty disguise

You call and I'd come even through the snowfall
No matter how frozen over the blood in my veins
The one promise I couldn't bring myself to break
Perhaps December is proof that endings can be beautiful

apathy

/ˈapəTHē/ noun

---

lack of feeling or emotion;
indifference

11:22 PM

I've always wondered why
Why you feign indifference
When you've never in your years
Been much good at pretending
Why do you hide?

When your every esoterica
Is as priceless a work as any
When it is a museum I see
Preserved through you
Why do you hide?

Perhaps you only claim apathy
For you feel so boundlessly
Perhaps your claims are so loud
So your feelings don't drown you
But you don't have to hide from me.

I will find a way to find you through deluge
I will find a way to let light fall upon
The shield of shadow enveloping you
I will not let you conceal yourself any longer
Because you don't have to hide from me.

I refuse to believe you feel nothing
for it is you who made me feel so much

apricity

/aprīcitāt-em/ noun

---

the warmth of the sun in winter

They saw you as winter
But I saw you as apricity

They couldn't see through
A shield as transparent as ice
And I could see through one
As blinding as sunlight

I can't even find comfort in looking
At the same constellations as them
There's too much fog in their sky
To see anything but Argentine haze

They say out of sight, out of mind
And even though you could never leave
I could never let you leave my mind's gaze
I stop blinking just in case

The only way I've ever seen myself
Has been through your wintry eyes
So I've stopped looking in the mirror
Till your sunlit soul meets mine

Because they saw you as winter
And I saw you as apricity

crestfallen

/ˈkres(t)ˌfôlən/ adjective

a feeling of dejection

3:08 AM

I whisper, "I've hated you forever"
And yet how could I ever
In a thousand forevers forget
I've loved you just as long?

I fear I've loved you too long
Too long and so much so
That it will take forever
To unlearn that love.

You left me in so many pieces
So crestfallen over your absence
That even if the world didn't end
My world did, then and there.

And yet, I refuse to break
Especially at your hands
No matter how desperately
I yearn for your touch.

incandescence

/ˌɪn.kænˈdes.əns/ noun

---

glowing or white with intense heat;
intensely bright or brilliant

4:11 AM

you ask me why I choose you
why I choose your tempest
choose the fall of your rain
over the incandescence of fire
over the glacial apathy of ice
you're hopeless, aren't you?
for despite it all, you fail to see
through your melancholy fog
that when fire and ice battle
pursuing the same conquest
it is your rain that reigns
it is your storm that is worthy
of fate's rapt attention
you are destiny's chosen
as much as you are mine
that is why I choose tempest
that is why I choose you

January

1:01 AM

January's fallen, shattered mirrorball
Reflects stories I'd rather leave untold
I'd have broken a thousand times
If it'd been you putting me back together

I could've lived and died on a pedestal
Of our stolen moments and illicit stares
For you were always at my forefront
Even as I tried to make you a footnote

Thanks to you, I can make poison my home
For once you were my home, poison was harmless
Now you can't even call me your biggest mistake
For I was never yours in the first place

I should thank you for cutting me open
For the blood that fell from my wounds
Was intrinsically bound to my words
It told more stories than I ever could

I'd always loved words until I realized
That's all you were; tears on paper
That's when actions became my sanctuary
And that's what I hated you for; my stolen words

I've never been able to deny you
Anything you ever asked of me
So in January I beg you to ask me to leave
For maybe then I'd finally be able to

limerence

/ˈlɪmɪrəns/ noun

a state of mind resulting from
romantic attraction, characterized
by feelings of euphoria; the desire to
have one's feelings reciprocated

4:09 AM

perhaps I never made you
a thousand paper cranes
for I knew you'd leave
long before I'd ever finish
for once I brought you wings
just to watch them burn
I am the pen through which
you bleed every midnight
that which you abandon
when the sun is back
upon its pedestal in the sky
and light hits crimson tones
isn't it romantic?
how I'm your one regret
your midnight love
your reckless abandon
the home you return to
when the sunlight
isn't there to watch
they all call it your loss
so why am I the one grieving?
am I your midnight love?
or your midnight limerence

niveous

/ˈnivēəs/ adjective

---

snowy or resembling snow

12:01 AM

shredded paper snow
a shroud of withered winter
think of a lie, pretty as snow
and watch as its two faces
go pale as wintry frost
in comparison to my firelit truth
even with its wax melted
reduced to all but a void
its glass cage black with ash
the candle's infallible truth
will never stop burning
even in shredded paper snow
a shroud of withered winter

sanity

/ˈsanədē/ noun

___

the ability to think and behave in a
normal and rational manner; sound
mental health.

12:30 AM

all my life
you claimed
all you wanted
was to see me smile
and yet in the end
it's always you
left smiling
as my tears fall
it's excruciating
till it isn't anymore
your laugh sounds
less like a laugh
more like a scream
that penetrates
all sane thought
that cuts through
any peace I've felt
till I'm left bleeding
with bloodshot eyes
and bloodless veins
piercing shadow
fearing footfall

tempest

/ˈtempəst/ noun

a violent and windy storm, usually
accompanied by rainfall

4:02 AM

They see the dark in your tempest
While my eyes reflect your light
And the formosity I see through the storm
Is enough to blind even lightning

You may be the chaos in the fire
But it is chaos that I crave, that calls to me
You're a storm I cannot escape
My heart echoes the chaos of your flames

You are more a part of me
Than water is of all the seven seas
And I would search for you in every life
Along every grain of sand in the desert

February

02:05 AM

February nights, fight or flight
You chose fight, as always
As I waited for my feelings to take flight
Leaving me behind at the terminal

Throughout a thousand lifetimes
I've slipped into life's shadow
Dictated by your uncertainty
Tainted by your indecision

And no matter how much I master
The art of packing my life into a suitcase
The panic, the dread, the emptiness
They require far too much space

So I pack them into my head
Into my heart and soul
Till I can breathe no longer
Suffocated despite abundant air

February days, spent in foreign lands
In foreign hearts and foreign minds
I've become inured to the emptiness
It is no longer a foreign land

Spring

March

3:18 AM

Fields of flowers fall from my eyes
And rivers dance at my fingertips
I tread fearlessly upon the sunlit sky
My face upturned towards rolling hills
For nothing has been as it was
As it would've, could've, should've been
Since you.

Head in the clouds and you on my mind
I only lose myself to my surroundings
In the hope that they'll find me somewhere
And once I find myself, perhaps I'll find you
Or perhaps if I fall in love with the heartbreak
It'll leave my life so blissfully, fearlessly
Like you did.

Your birthday etched into my memory
The memory of your melody on the wind
March blooms as you let me wilt
You were the Sun and perhaps I got too close
For I felt the burn as you scorched my skin
I felt the moment the Atlantic burst into flames
Another reminder of you.

amaranthine

\am-uh-RANTH-un\ adjective

---

of or relating to an amaranth;
eternal or undying

4:15 AM

from place to place
from Vienna to Versailles
a solitary traveler I remain
yet you are the one place
I could never leave
the sole reckless abandon
that I could never abandon
for I found home
I found sanctuary
in the solace of your voice
for we are amaranthine
I'll forever be your moon
you'll be my muse; my entire sky
I was forever lost to you
long before our eyes met
I was nameless long before
you named me forever yours

deluge

/ˈdelˌyōoj/ noun

---

a severe flood or heavy fall of rain

I could see through you
long before you knew
the color of my eyes
long before you witnessed
the forget-me-nots
unfurl in my gaze
it is only through your lens
that even something
as scandalously futile as life
can seem an adversary
worthy of your attention
every part of me aches
to carry your soul with me
as the wind carries with it
all your dandelions
my ink tries to fall into place
as hard as my hands try
to leave imprints on your heart
yet both fail so miserably
for my words aren't worthy of you
and my hands cannot hold back
they will not ever hold back
such a violently stunning deluge

desiderium

/desəˈdirēəm/ noun

---

an ardent desire or longing

2:09 AM

When I tell you all about
my greatest heartbreak
one that left me devastated
ruined, yearning in its absence
I ask you not to be blinded
by all your boundless pity
for knowing such heartbreak
knowing such pure desiderium
means I've known love
just as intimately
even if it left my soul
scattered in irrecoverable pieces
each piece still yearned for it
each piece still yearns for you
I yearn for the one thing
that left me broken
for it is the one thing
that has the power to ruin me
and the power to heal me just as well

devastation

/ˌdevəˈstāSH(ə)n/ noun

---

severe destruction or damage;
overwhelming shock or grief

8:15 PM

I refuse to acknowledge
The echoes of your bloodshed
Refuse to be bonded by that bloodshed
And just because you can't hear me
Over your own relentless screams
Doesn't mean I'm not screaming
Just as relentlessly as you are

I refuse to fight this war with you
For I'm already preoccupied
By the one fought within
And if everything I gave
Truly wasn't enough for you?
Then perhaps 'enough'
Is not what I wish to be any longer

To satisfy your thirst for blood
I'd have to change every aspect
Every intricacy of my being
Till I can recognise myself no longer
And I'd rather be myself
Than the version of me
You'd force yourself to care for

Blood may run thicker than water
Yet only water can quench my thirst
Only love can quench the war you've waged
I will wait, patiently, till rain comes
Till it heals the ravaged land you've left
Till all blood from the battlefield
Is finally washed away with the tide

April

4:14 AM

April stole away my words
For why write about someone
Why immortalize someone
Who is bound to one day be
Unworthy of such words
Of such unconditional devotion
And yet, blood always flows
Freely from an open wound
In April, I claim you lost me
The second that first tear fell
I hate you, I confide in April
You say it back like an oath
We're both fools, aren't we?
Relying on truth to conceal secrets
When truth is all that secrets are
I refuse to apologize for hurting you
The scars from the wounds you gave
Will simply never allow me to
Perhaps there is strength in our scars
And unyielding weakness in our stars
Our present is what history once was
To think of you every time
The first note in our symphony plays
That is my eternal burden to bear
Isn't it beautiful, I ask April
How your own memories replace you
Loving you is the one nightmare
We both refuse to wake up from
And perhaps I find comfort
In the weight of your malice
For it is all but a reprieve from
The weightlessness of your love

facade

/fəˈsäd/ noun

---

an outward appearance that is
maintained to conceal a less
pleasant reality

3:24 AM

Talking to you was my safe haven
It came as naturally as the beat of breath
And I've deprived myself of oxygen
I've suffocated without you far too long

I claimed to have you locked out
Banished from my heart mind and soul
Yet even after all those years and tears shed
The key still lies in your hands

Even as your words pierced my heart
Even as you threw them at me
With no remorse, no regrets
All I could do was praise your aim

As you twisted the knife, as you ruined my life
I stood there smiling as I bled for you
Because a life ruined by you
Was far better than a life without you

Why did it take me so many lifetimes?
Memories wasted to disentangle your facade
I trace it on my skin, along my sorrowful words
I let my own heart fall and shatter just to catch yours

I loved you like oxygen and that is why
I've stopped breathing

hiraeth

/hiːraɪθ/ noun

---

a homesickness for a home which
you cannot return to or that never
was; intense yearning for home

my mind's eye forever blind
lost in crimson haze
love or fury everlasting
as much as I defy it
the difference defines me
it is painful how my pain
is a reminder of your eyes
eyes that asked me why
I couldn't tell you I loved you
how could I ever explain
the agony of longing
for something I already have
or perhaps something
that was never mine at all
you say you love flowers
so you take enough
to last you forever
that love is why they die
that love is as much their end
as it always has been ours
and perhaps that is why
my mind refuses to love
what my heart already does
perhaps that is why
you can never be my home
only my everlasting hiraeth

symphony

/ˈsimfənē/ noun

---

an elaborate musical composition
for full orchestra; a harmonious
arrangement

you ask why I'd cut off my ears
before listening to 'our song' again
why I would slit my throat
before singing it for you again
clearly you never lost your mind
consumed by the devastation
clearly you never truly loved
for if you had, you would know
listening to the symphony of us
would make the notes conform
to the sorrowful shape of my voice
rivers would flow from your ears
there'd be thunder in your throat
that is why it is now so clear
you never lost your mind over me
you never truly, unconditionally loved
for you've never experienced
your soul being cleaved in two
and a part of you letting it shatter
and perhaps I pity you for it all
for not only have you never loved
you've never been loved just the same

unconditional

/ˌənkənˈdiSH(ə)nəl/ adjective

---

not subject to any conditions;
absolute and limitless

9:02 PM

the memory of you
now stitched in my veins,
in my torn up words
my bared and broken soul
you are the tears and fears
beyond my years
the tapestry of your life
irreversibly weaved into mine
so irrevocably
that I couldn't let you go
even if I managed
to bring myself to try
you are - were - mine
unconditionally mine

May

5:10 AM

Isn't it sad, beautiful, tragic?
How May evenings may pity me
The girl who had home in every place
Left with home as but a poor facade

For one knows me all too well
Knows my red haze and starry gaze
In its soil lies my soul, every epiphany
It remembers so well all I hope to forget

The other knows me not well enough
It knows not how my tears form words
How my words shape my tears
All it knows is cold indifference

Perhaps that is why I call neither home
For home is all but a fabled myth
For I know to be peregrine all too well
Too well to ever know to be home

Summer

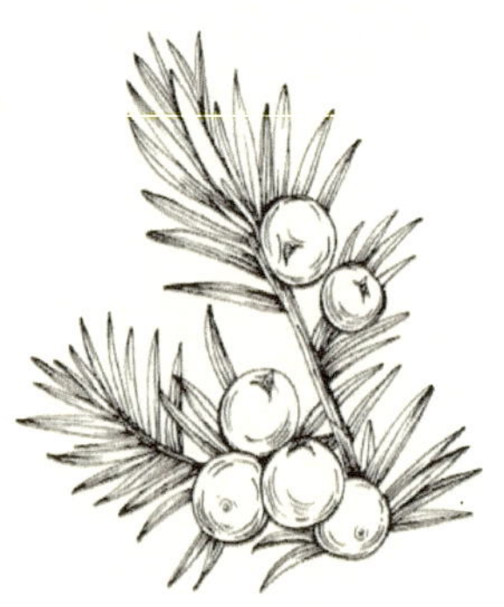

June

12:21 AM

"Meet me by the juniper"
You asked of me in June
How was I ever to know
You waited by the belladonna
Perhaps our juniper tree
Was barren for a reason
Perhaps because in summer
I asked you to turn the car left
But you just left me instead
You claimed so righteously
That the difference departed
Even far long after it set
Long after the sky's eye closed
You blamed your blindness
On the sun's superficial scandal
You blamed your blindness
On poisoned truth and pretty lies
On sunless sights and sunlit nights
On anything, everything but you
On anything, everything but June

atlantis

/æt'læntɪs/ noun

(in ancient legend) a mythical
continent said to have sunk beneath
the Atlantic Ocean

11:07 PM

I'd find a way if you asked
To breathe underwater for you
All you ever had to do
Was ask me not to drown

I search for you in every place
I chase the myth of you
Like a madman in search
Of the lost city of Atlantis

I'll always choose the myth of you
Over the reality of anyone else
For my soul seeks out yours
Like land to the seven seas

aureate

/ˈôrēət,ˈôrēˌāt/ adjective

denoting, made of, or having the
color gold

10:22 PM

My camera may capture
city lights
But my wandering eyes
capture you
I told you I loved gold
and you gave me
a gold mine
I could have the world
at my feet
And still be lost in thoughts
of you
I could have the stars
in my hands
And still think of nothing but
your eyes
My foolish heart
grows jealous
Of the space you take up
in my head
And even as my throat
grows hoarse
My pages scream
your name
For you are as aureate
as city lights.

catalyst

/ˈkadləst/ noun

a person or thing that causes a
change or event to happen

1:16 AM

A part of me wishes
That I had it in me to wish
But perhaps the stars
Have had enough

I'm at chance's precipice
Past and future converge
For I don't experience time
I live and breathe it

The son of Phanes
The daughter of Keres
I'd abandon death's door
Abandon dusk for your dawn

You are just as addicting
As you are addicted to torment
You are as much my catalyst
As you are my calamity

cicatrised

/ˈsikəˌtrīz/ verb

____

to close or be closed by scar
formation; heal

3:08 AM

you cry a sea of tears
all for fate's sympathy
even though I'm the one
you gave all your scars

you claim you're burning
that your flesh is on fire
even though I'm the one
whose life you left in ashes

from me you wanted silence
and yet, when your desire fulfilled
when my heart gave you silence
you relented like you never asked for it

once I abandon you like you did me
I hope I leave your memory entirely
for you do not deserve to have me at all
even in the confines of your thoughts

it was all too exhausting, you claim
to raise the sun from the dead at dawn
even as it was you who buried it
you who desired sunlight all at once

your pained anguish flickers
in and out as fate comes and goes
I'm the one who keeps burning
all thanks to your lack of light

you wanted my pain to glimmer
like some twisted trophy of hurt
what you wanted was myth's daughter
I will not apologize for being reality's

July

7:23 PM

July evenings infused with halcyon
Blind to the beginning of our end
We were incendiary enough
To send even flame into frenzy

You were a fire at the oceanside
You know it was never in your heart
Never written in your veins
To be a flame cold as ice

Perhaps you were my problem
But at least in July you were mine
The sun stayed upon its pedestal
The moon listened through our rendezvous

Long story short, we stood at the edge
We fell hopelessly in august
Reached impact in September
But July was imbued with our oblivion

eclipsed

/əˈklips/ verb

(of a celestial body) obscure or
block out light

_8:02 PM_

she wishes to glow
underneath sunlight
neglecting the fact
that she is the sun
it's difficult not to fall
fall in love with her
so hopelessly
so irrevocably
under eventide
that all else remains
eclipsed in her shadow
it is evident that her light
has blinded you
for no matter
how many constellations
no matter how many stars
I have to offer
they're never
magnificent enough

ephemeral

/əˈfem(ə)rəl/ adjective

something that is fleeting or short-lived; temporary

3:17 AM

I hope those fleeting, ephemeral moments
Were worth losing the one and only person
Who would've lit a fire in the ocean for you
Was losing forever worth momentary pleasure?

I hope you drown in your boundless sea of hurt
As I willfully revoke all lifelines handed to you
I hope you drown in your ocean of regret
As every lighthouse is felled by your presence

You tried to ruin us and it is now your ruination
I cross your name once, cross it twice in my list
Till each letter is as twisted, as ruined in my head
As the contemptful thoughts going through yours

Perhaps the poets were right in their words
Distance makes the heart grow fonder, surely
For I am a thousand times fonder of your absence
Than I was of your illicit affairs and vile fabrications

Under sunlight, shadows form; that is where you strike
So isn't it fair for me to reside under the cover of night?
We built an empire, but I will not search for you in its ashes
For it is now your end that marks my beginning.

evanescence

/ɛvəˈnɛsɪns/ noun

---

the quality of being fleeting or
vanishing quickly; impermanence

6:24 AM

I am the evanescence of a pendulum
A constant back and forth
From person to person and back
From place to place and back

I am the sand that falls into the ocean
And then finds its way back to shore
I am the wind that leaves in august
And returns with a force in December

In my voice you hear the in and out of breath
In my breath you hear call and response
In the evanescence of my fate you hear
Falling; of snow to sun, of leaves to rain

In the beat of my footsteps you hear
The ticking down of a timer
You listen to my heart beat and stop
Time of death, 6:24 AM.

lovelorn

/ˈlʌv.lɔːrn/ adjective

bereft of love or of a lover; suffering
from unrequited love

They say that it is beyond possibility
To feel more heartbreak than love-
For it is love that welcomes heartbreak
Nothing but lies, as the heartbreak is all I recall

They say to love is to relinquish all control
To let yourself fall into the dark, blind with trust
And with no hesitation, if I were given a choice
I'd choose control over love forevermore

Because long after love leaves you
Alone with unwanted remembrances
Lost in starless depths and sunless days
It is control that will console you

Under nightfall and shattered starlight
Even in the depths of heartbreak undesired
Even as love leaves you drunk on memories lost
Control is all that love could never be

August

11:02PM

We're so far from august, aren't we?

My tears fell and you blamed me for the salt in the air
Even as I broke parts of myself to fix you
Even as I stopped my heart to revive one that'd stopped beating
Hoping against all hope what'd died wouldn't stay dead
Hoping against hope that august would be ours forevermore

I stood between the ashes of a past only half mine
Clinging desperately to embers lost in the wind
I clung to those embers defiantly even as I burned
Even as the bonfire died down, the memories lived
And so I stayed in august, right where you left me

I watched my reflection in your eyes as you left
And I saw two people I couldn't recognise
You came and went like august, and I waited still
I stood with time till it one day grew tired and left
Leaving nothing but memories I'd rather forget

And so I stand, with unspoken words and untold stories
At the grave of someone who isn't even dead
You come and go as you please and I burn each time
Yet I still cling to embers of our past and the cycle repeats
Until I can't tell which one of us is walking away

We're so far from august, aren't we?

Autumn

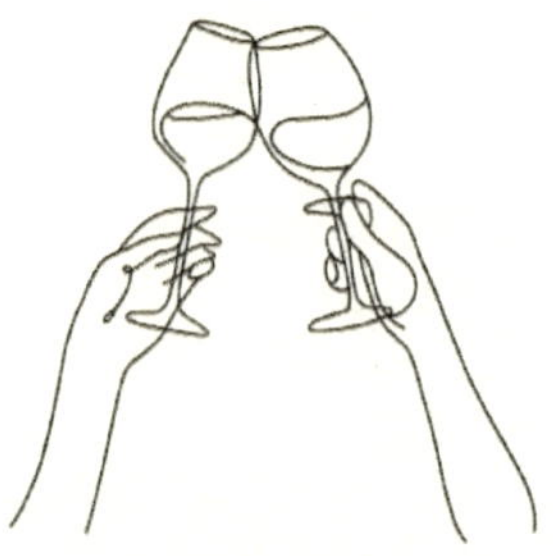

September

2:26 AM

I stood by your side through the darkest of night
To watch you betray me in broad daylight
I watched from behind yellow tape titled 'caution'
Wishing I'd seen the signs and left when I had the chance
I watched as you ruined memories still only half yours

I died so many deaths by your spoken words
So many lifetimes ended by your untold stories
My life was empty far before you took me to my grave
And I wait behind veils of malice for justice to find you
I wait for peace to betray you, like you did me

And when I bring you what you brought upon yourself
Death by a thousand cuts will be a sweet mercy
From the agony of forevermore without me spent
Alone with your pretty lies spun behind my back
And ugly truths unopened at my doorstep

And now I blissfully embrace September evenings
As you remain stranded in august nights without starlight
I listen to our symphony until it makes me sick
As you pine for what you know you lost so long ago
You stay right where I left you as I walk away smiling

As you remain all but a transient phase in my moments
The thought of you slowly becomes ephemeral
For if you had the time to pick and choose
Which parts of me were worthy of your attention
Your attention wasn't worth my time to begin with

callosity

/kəˈläsədē/ noun

---

the quality or state of being callous,
hardened, or unfeeling

2:27 AM

Second choice is a setting at the table reserved for me
But never at any dinners you were at until now
And no matter how long I scramble for purchase
It feels like I'm falling off a ledge of my own making
I've found my peace in being the second ♦ choice
At every table, except for yours
I would rather fall than be your backup
Fighting a battle I can never win
In a war I created by finding you a first choice
An opponent unaware she's in combat
I can't afford to give you my all again
Just to watch you hand out our downfall
I would rather walk away with my bleeding heart
Than go back to two with such blinding callosity
I am done trying to live up to your first choice
I will not be second for another second of our story

catharsis

/kəˈTHärsəs/ noun

---

the process of releasing, and
thereby providing relief from, strong
or repressed emotions

4:29 AM

The water rises and falls
Our fountain's breath
Rages as rampant as mine

Where the solemn rain reigns
My heart hopelessly hopes to trace
Where the droplets meet your skin

I yearn to be your storm's light
To be the solitude in the sky
Reflected in your eyes

With every heartbeat I ache
To be the one to see you alight
Alight as the lightning does

It is catharsis I crave; I call out to
It is in sunlight that bodies bask
Yet it is in tempest's time that I thrive

epiphany

/əˈpifənē/ noun

a moment of sudden revelation or
insight

4:10 AM

Under the flickering night
Your eyes alight by the fireside
Irises turned molten in the dusk
Lit by the seraphic sun

Memories of moonlight escape you
Blinded by the boundless sunlight
If the memories haven't killed you yet
Perhaps they've made you immortal

Perhaps the moon only hates you
Because of the embers in your eyes
The embers that stayed just the same
Even as you changed with the fall

Perhaps the moon was your eternal
Your secrets fated to the stars
But the sun was your epiphany
Your promises lost with eventide

esoterica

/iːsəˈtɛɹɪkə/ noun

---

things understood by or meant for a
select few; recondite matters or
items

3:31 AM

isn't it tragic that you
cannot see through my eyes
isn't it tragic that you
hide your chaos so vigilantly
behind veiled shadows

isn't it tragic how you don't know
that you are the most magnificent thing
I've ever witnessed
isn't it tragic how you don't know
that you are the kind of esoterica
people wage wars and create art over

it is not tragic that you are my muse
it is tragic that you'll never know
that you've been immortalized

October

12:16 AM

Leaves have veins but no heart
And yet they still keep falling
And of course our two hearts
Are fated to fall with them

Every clandestine October night
I find my way through the foliage
Under the weight of our downfall
Under the chains of fallen tears

I wonder if it is the fallen leaves
That shatter beneath my footsteps
Or if it is the broken remnants of us
That fragment and fracture so willingly

Through the haze, amber eyes follow me
I could fall into Autumn's dulcet voice
It haunts me as much as yours does
You were my equinox and I waited for you

Wrapped in whispers of autumnal chill
I whisper a thank you to our fallen tears
They gave me something to blame you for
For blaming fate was never enough for me

fable

/ˈfāb(ə)l/ noun

a false, fictitious, or improbable
account; a story or legend

4:30 AM

I miss moments before they end
I miss people before they leave
Leave blissfully in darkness and light
That is why it all fades to grey

How can I so fearlessly blame fate
When it is my own faith to blame?
I am the harbinger of my own downfall
The idea of home is my faithful fable

I would've given you my words; my world
All you ever had to do was ask
I was a fool; unknowing you'd take it
Whether I was willing or not

I crossed the transom
You called for my ransom
But I had nothing left to give
Only so much left to forget

I never had a chance, did I?
Not after past and future stilled
Never after your words were my end
After I lived to feel the death you bestowed

It is as much a blessing as your curse
To never see my wistful eyes
When they're searching for you
For I know now not to search for a myth

luminary

/ˈluː.mə.ner.i/ adjective

---

of, involving, or characterized by
light or enlightenment

2:16 AM

you yearn for the stars
who welcome the moon
who accept an outsider
you yearn for luminescence
although you are luminary
you are a supernova
the kind of light one has
only after breaking
you dream of starry eyes
of starswept nights
and yet, it is called
starcrossed for a reason
those stars are the same
that'd forsake the sun
so willingly abandon
one of their own

petrichor

/ˈpetrĭˌkôr/ noun

---

the earthy scent produced by and
associated with rainfall

2:04 AM

Isn't it beautiful?
How my eyes meet yours
How they'd always find you
Even if I were blind
Captivated yet held captive
I feed the fire oxygen
In hopes it'll extinguish
But the flames only grow
They spread till we're a wildfire
Till even the rain
Is all but falling flame
You are the water in my veins
And the blood in my tears
You are the air in the ocean
And the petrichor in the air
You are the fault line
Where fire and rain meet
Everywhere, everything all at once

transience

/ˈtran(t)SHəns/ noun

---

the state or fact of lasting only for a
short time; transitory nature

9:19 PM

You showed me the kind of love
The poets write sonnets about
I defended your honor tirelessly
Like a soldier defending his homeland
You were a map; mine to conquer
A kingdom the king was envious of

And yet, in love and in war
There is bone crushing heartbreak
There is a peace that envelops battle
Every conquest is simply transient

You left me devastated enough
To earn the poets' pitiful gaze
You left me in enough agony
That even the soldier surrendered
You left me broken enough
That even the king bowed before me

November

4:20 AM

you were never a promise
made to break ever so easily
you were an immortal oath
bloodbound by my heartbeat
I was wistful melancholy
and you were my solace
I chose November nights with you
not because I had no choice
rather because it is your eyes
that I saw amidst the candlelight
your voice was my lighthouse
you called to me, steadfast
through all the bottomless depths
of seven seas worth of torment
you are forevermore the only one
I would follow to winter's precipice

Acknowledgements

A huge thank you to my parents, for the experiences I wouldn't have been able to write this book without, for the hours spent designing and publishing, and the constant support; and to my brother, for the patience when I disappeared into my own world for hours on end.

To every single friend who's made it this far, thank you so much for being my safe space, my late-night inspiration, and the people I'm proud to call 'my people.' You've listened through my endless rants and drafts no matter what time it was, and no matter how long I went on about things you didn't understand; thank you.

To every poet and writer whose words inspired me— there are far too many to name, and if I try the acknowledgments may be longer than the book —whether you know it or not, you taught me the beauty of vulnerability and the power in the words so many of us often take for granted.

To every experience, every word, and every muse- whether I've loved you, lost you, or taken you for granted, it meant enough for you to find yourself written between the pages of this book; so, thank you, because my words are nothing without the meaning you've given to them.

Finally, to my readers: thank you for holding this book in your hands. Your willingness to step into my world, even for a moment, means everything. This is for you—the people who dare to dream, and those who find poetry in the gap between every heartbeat.

— Suhani

www.ingramcontent.com/pod-product-compliance
Lightning Source LLC
Chambersburg PA
CBHW022032150726
47990CB00002B/921